Rummaged Runes
The Poem Pack

Flairs and Glairs
Publication House

"Rummaged Runes"

ISBN No: " 978-93-90799-36-7"
1st Edition
Language – English

Flairs and Glairs
Publication House
Regd. Under MSME Act.

Disclaimer

This is a work of fiction and solely represent the thoughts of the corresponding author of the articles.
Our editors have tried their best to edit the content of all the authors and check the plagiarism.
All the write-ups in this book are unique and are only published in this book.
In case any plagiarism or error is found, only the author is responsible alone, and not the publisher.

Cover Designing and Book Formatting
Shubham Shah

Foreword

Words always come out of emotions, this is known to all, yet we see some manipulated stuff as well. But this book is purely from heart. It can be understood so easily, if read with that vision. The book offers content from various fields of feelings but each explained so well that you can experience the life of the writer. The book gives an idea of how the writer perceives life and it's different flavours. Each poem written in the book shows the intimacy between the writer, words and the writer's life. The circumstances that are in the form of poetry in the book are known to all but only a writer can explain all of that in such a beautiful way. It feels so good to read quality content written so well.

The writer has tried to share her experiences through poetry. Each word seems to come from her heart. We can have an idea of her life just by reading this book. It contains all the themes that should be included.

To feel something is fine, but to express what you feel is a task that our generation usually avoids. The book has been presented with a hope, that we get practiced to the fact expressing yourself is normal and it should be done. In other case, you may lead to mental destruction.

~Maleeha sofi

Acknowledgement

Writing has always been my passion, but still, it is never so easy to succeed in what you desire or crave for. Same is the story with me. My life has been a kind of roller coaster to accomplish whatsoever I have done till date. My zeal for writing and the peace that came along with it, has played a key role in this book. Of course, nothing would have been possible if Almighty; the all Powerful, had not been merciful enough, whenever I felt like giving up. Living in a society with high critiques, my parents, Altaf Ahmed Lone and Saira Lone have been a backbone for me. They have stood by my side through every thick and thin, even when I thought I didn't need their help. I can't resist my pen to mention my best buddies, my siblings whom I consider a blessing from My Creator; especially, Ayaan and Arab. Besides, I could have never stood here without the support of a few of my companions who have been my strength whenever I was living at my lowest. A huge thanks to my helping hands, including Jahangir Lone, Javid Rather, Mohsin Ali, Maleeha Sofi, Hinna Bhat , B Huzaif Bukhari, Wani Aasef, Sahiba Iqbal and Sania Parray It's well said that, 'Every expert was once a beginner.' and I feel myself blessed enough to start as a beginner at Budding Bloom Experimental School Baramulla. They have taught me lessons more than academics, that keep me going.

In general, I want to extend my heartfelt note of thanks to everyone who prayed for me and has either supported me or been against me. Yes, a special thanks to those who always had tried to bring me down because I got to know my height only when I was pulled down.

And finally, SHE discerns;
Neither her dismaying look nor her
glamour, but it was her integrity
that made him fall for her,
He fell for her soul before he could
feel her.
If this was not love, then what else
is?

Ayieena Altaf

.

Contents

Resilient Mother

Everyday is a day of joy; as she teaches them,
Giving her own voice; that's how her days were spent.
The little hands she safely held, as they walked together and sled,
Nourishing those little buds; emotionally before they fled.
Teaching them the courage and not to cow;
To share and to be kind and fair and to bow.
Oh soon, what becomes of a mother's despair?
Dreaming of their future; starry and bright
But one got killed in a blurry fight.
That prompted the other to become a rebel.
Placed arms on his shoulders; oh what a cruelly miserable fable!
Yet another was interrogated time and again,
Tears fell from her eyes like the never stopping rain.
Her hopes got dashed in this long oppression;
Countless mothers have lost their lovely creation.
Graveyard is overfilled, Where the innocent souls are killed.
Nobody seems to care, no human life is billed.
For every MOTHER her son is rare,
Other than humans, everything seems valuable here.
She bore pain more than anyone can realize.
We cannot count how much she had to compromise.

Matriarch

For all the love you gave me every day,
In place of every sadness that you threw away.
The little hands you safely hold,
And all the rules that infinite times you told.
For being there with me;
I am thankful and will always be.
For all the alluring things that you do,
that helped me all the year through.
Every day you taught me is a day of elation.
For you, I have my own expressions.
You believe me more than I believe in myself .
And do more for me than I do for myself.
For giving me birth, you bore so much pain,
It is a burden to carry that no one else can.
For you make me shine everywhere,
You are the one to me, my most dear.

Alter Ego

You are never far from me, always in my heart,
I wish God would never keep us apart.
For, like little babies when we cry,
you hug us tenderly, indefinite is your love supply.
We feel each other's joy and share each other's pain
We love each other like no one can.
Our lives were brought together earlier,
for if you are with me, fear exists nowhere.
Now I am grown up you still treat me like a kid.
Someone I can call when things don't go right.
With you, my life is shiny and bright.
When I fall down you help me to rise up
without you I feel so much out of luck.
The one that stands for me among all the other rest,
Is one and only; my sister and my very best.
You are like a bright shining star that forever shine,
You are one of the greatest gifts, and forever mine.
There is space in my Heart where you stay,
An unconditional love that won't go away.
You are my faithful partner till the end,
this bond is straight, and will never bend.

It Would Engulf Yet I Would Crave

The tighter you clutch me in your arms,
The more the crave is risen in all forms.
 All over and everywhere;
There is no other craving left elsewhere.
Your love has such an implication,
It engulfs me and I know no limitation.
I long for you intensely,
And love you forever immensely.
My soul is whirling on your pole Faster and faster like the spinning wheel,
I want to be lost in you whole, And from there never to unseal.

Poetess

She is a poetess,
A blessing to beckon Words can't express; Such is her tune.
She is a dewdrop
In the morning rose, Shimmering top on top Eschews repose.
She writes by the ink of her heart, sings odes of her soul,
Thinks a limpid thought; oh, her eyes never ole.
Each of her word is a drop of truth,
Lavish melody and verses; and never uncouth.
She is a shining star in my vast sky, Brighter than days are her ways.

A Secret She Keeps!

When her eyes met thine,
She found her heaven around
Guess, all her wishes slipped to heaven,
And she found them all when he was around.
She thought magic existed nowhere,
Then she met him & the rest is History.
He is forever settled in her heart,
 Loving him was natural to her,
 Forgetting him was equally Unnatural,
Where did he go, in the land pastoral?

Will you ever forgive me?

I seek apologies that I didn't loved you, the way you deserved
I feel sorry for not listening to your feelings; that died hard.

So busy I was healing the bruises of others, while keeping mine afresh,
Thinking about the regrets, the pain makes me depressed.
I feel Sorry for letting you to pick others up,
And now you are gone; I want to interrupt!
I seek apologies for letting you cry when I was wiping tears of others,
Forcing you to laugh, when we both felt like losers.
You didn't had mood to spread that curve,
I didn't have the courage to hug you, and not that nerve.
I feel sorry to waste my time and love for the ones who didn't know how to return,
I never knew life would take such a U-turn!
I feel Sorry for not letting you sleep and keep you awakened to the wails of others.
I feel Sorry for not giving you strength when you were all for yourself.
I feel Sorry for not consoling you when you were lying on the Floor.
I seek apologies for not taking your side.
Will you ever forgive me?

Race by Face

This world boasts of a race
Where we are judged as per our face
That's how our colours are made
Slipping Good and bad in our fate

Although they still outlast
On the basis of caste,
Where humanity is just a name
The world of minds portrays every different frame.
God painted the humans with divine colors, White,
black, brown so on,
To fill the garden of flowers, Relish the vibrancy of
the lawn.
Mankind, that is still asleep, must wake and
understand
That our hearts and souls are same in this wonderland
This race and caste
No more in the beauty fall
They are faint minds who outlast, and never grow tall.
One must quit the mind of difference, and admit
God's glance
Gaze through the eyes of the heart
And praise the Lord's Art.

The Childhood Home

Every morning I wake, the only wish I make,
I wish I could be little again, have my school days back.
Where is that road that I cannot track?
I wish I could attend that melodious Morning assembly again,
The teachings that were good for my brain.
Thinking about the first day i stepped into my school,
When we thought we were being so cool.
Thinking about those carefree days makes me a little sad,
How the beloved teachers held our hands like mom and dad.
Thank you, teacher, for always doing your best to stimulate your knowledge and Entrust.
The school taught me what was essential,
That's how I became closer to my aim and potential.
Now, even when I am no more a part of my school
For me, it will always be the best place and a magic tool.
Those picnic memories are still afresh.
Looking at those childhood pictures makes my face blush.
 I always wish my school to rock and Bloom.
Calling its name is Honor, that's Budding bloom.

Broken Mirror

She used a broken piece of mirror,
Just to see an errorless face
She wanted to find the errors
But there was only grace;
Although the pain was wrapped in the loomed cloth,
Something dangerous had happened, to the heart and soul both.
Oh! Brutally she held the mirror in her hand
And watched for hours and hours,
No scars, no wounds, only tearful showers.

I Lost My Childhood

To the child in me
I want to discern you once more, When I was in your company,
I used to do witless things,
I was free from all frets,
Full day amusement, no cutbacks,
Unaware about the concept of lies, and cheating
When life was just a beautiful greeting.
When it was possible to Live blithely,
Where the moon rose high, and the sun shone brightly.
When Pleasure meant being surrounded by kids,
When disjunction meant grappling with Friends,
When cheating meant purloining coins.
When dreams meant going outside on weekends.
When lies meant an excuse to skip school.
Yes, I lost that precious stage
Oh! How I am living now, what is this age?

She Lost Her Soul

She is at that stage of life
Where the life reads a page
Where her mind guide's her to the reality,
And where the heart fearlessly flee.
Her heart continues to bleed,
She wants to move on,
but the heart doesn't pay any heed.

Teary eyes, agony filled heart and fake smiles is all
that is left
No purpose in life, all blessing bereft

She lost her soul for long
In a fight between the mind and the heart forlorn

Her story doesn't end here
oh! how she had fantasized its song.
It charts among the stories,
Whose climax rips off one's heart?

Delves

What shall I do with these tears?
that keeps trickling down my face?
What shall I do with this broken heart?
Beats missing; try and, listen; it's a world apart.
What shall I do with this time?
It is running at its pace but I'm standing aloof; even
in springtime.
What shall I do with this rose?
It talks about your beauty and the fate that I chose.
What shall I do with this tongue?
Your lyrics strung to it and the praises clung.
What should I do with those roads?
That left me thinking at crossroads.
What shall I do with my dream?
Where I see the future dull and bleak.
What shall I do of these relationships that are ended
by the silence?
I cannot live in this darkness,
Let's go and bring back those dawns again.
Life without your, is dull land artless.

Slipping Love

You are trying to omit me.
How can you?
How can you omit that moment when,
You said that I make your life ravishing?
How can you?
How can you omit those imbecile jokes we used to crack to make each other laugh?
Now sitting on the bench in the park, I laugh at your behalf.
How can you omit those childish activities of mine which made you fall for me?
Taking care of each other, and talking endlessly under the birch tree.
It was you, who told me no matter what;
I will always hold your mitt and it is you who is trying hard to omit me, you forgot?
It is easy for you.
I was euphoric with you.
Now I only found your footprints imprinted on the wall of my heart.
Don't tell me our ways are different, and we have to part.
Our relationship is nameless I agree.
I know you are swamping, but I have to go with the wind, but the memories flee.
If I jump to save you,
Will you pull me down to stay?
If you ever see me smiling don't think I don't care, that's all I had to say.

Ayieena Altaf | 14

Now You Are Gone

You were my everything and now you are gone.
I lack the strength to carry on.
Sky always smiled when you were there,
but nothing is here now, in my sphere.
I love you so much for that, you were all I had.
But now there is nothing beyond depression; the reality is so sad.
When I met you, I knew not, we could go this far with our love and compassion, farther than far.
You took me to the world that was quite my own,
Moon twinkled there and the shining stars.
You made me what I could ever become.
Now you are not there I can't breathe I can't hum.
 Loving you is my passion ever, ever, and ever.
 No matter you are not here, I will love you forever and ever and ever.
I could have stayed but you left me in the abyss.
I can still see you, feel you, here you & it's my bliss.
But you became silent, my memories; you dismissed.

Precious Feelings

He can feel my tears and he doesn't want me to cry!
Yet I am crying because those precious feelings have
to die.

Sufficing

Not all the dreams you dream, come true.
Not everything you ever craved for; you get.
Not everything you seek, you would find.
Not everything you want, would seek your way.
You win, you don't keep your head up.
You don't have to stop the flow of water, simply fall
in Love with Life.

Memories

As I entered the room, I saw my dad crying.
As I asked him why was he crying?
He answered while masked,
"I recapitulate those spheres when they were burying my dad,
I was staring his dead body; waiting him to wake up and nod his head"
I asked a man, with all my profound pain,Why are you placing my Abba in soil?
They told me he will never wake up again,
Angrily, since I was on him; I looked at him in disdain.
I went to the graveyard to talk to him, waiting for his response in vain.
But he never replied, nor woke up;
I wrote my name there and returned home,
Everything seemed bleak, every place looked like a sad dome.
At last tears in our eyes sustain,
He told me nothing lasts forever only the memories remain.

Story of Heart

Don't ask the condition of my heart, Love!
I have a heart that beats like yours.
With every beat, it takes your name until hours.
I have a heart where you stay,
See, you are still here after you betray!
I have a heart which is broken,
It still keeps dreaming about you; while you are taken.
I have a heart which you call your home
while loving you I listen to my heart not dome.
I have a heart which is lost in mischief,
You don't know the depth of my love; but let me tell you in brief.

My Praised Poetry

He was never meant to be a Book or a Chapter,
For me; he is a Flower in search of nectar .
Verses and Rhyme; maybe
Or Feeings and Sign; maybe
Words And Lines is he
More than Couplets and Poems is he.
Tale and story is he
Indeed! A Beautiful and Limped glory is he
Yes My praised Poetry is he!

Ayieena Altaf | 20

Bitter Reality!

And we are all just fighting to survive in a world,
Where separation tells us the importance of a person.
Pain tells us the feelings of a person.
Tears tell us the story of this heart.
Poverty tells us the need for Prayers.
Morning tells us about regrets.
Where we hate the people, who treat us right.
And, only Hard situations remind us of Allah.

Self

I am a person, none I depend on,
Because I am not as I used to be,
I don't trust people anymore since the dawn,
because they only walk overly.
I have realized I am me,
And loving myself is my only aim,
I don't tell my secrets to any.
Distance myself from people because I know their games.
They will crush me and put all their blames.
When I start suffocating, I lock myself in the washroom
Then in the mirror, I look, and cry at a Low volume.
When I feel tired,I wipe my tears and come out
That's what I was looking to be admired for, and quit myself from lout.
I have become the person I depend upon no one.
I am looking for no one to fill my ocean.

Love Bear

Teddy bear, teddy bear
Listen to me,
You are my friend, my dear
All the way with me.

Beside my bed you stand
Silent and calm
When no one does understand
I clutch you in my arm.

You are sweet, cute
Buddy buddy i say,
Kufukakato your name on flute
I love to play.

Through the nights when alone
I hold beside me
Together we catch stars and moon
And live happy.

Teddy teddy, o my buddy
On your birthday,
Look at me and see
I have for you much to say.

Happy I Am Still.

I am all alone,
Happy I am, it's my fortune,
I pretend to be so,
When you are not even around; to show.
It makes me feel bound,
At times of meeting with anyone I feel unsound.
But yeah, I still Smile,
But looking at that mirror, I feel fragile.
Then again, the game begins with smiling and pretending.

Eyes Talk!

"Oh" the pain filled moment,
Staring in the mirror with Tears in eyes,
The eyes devoid of the dank colossal lies,
What is left to give?
Your eyes gave a Reason to Live!

Rest in Peace!

You are in pain.
You are feeling low.
You are getting mad for no reason; You are Sad.
You are confused.
You don't care about this world.
You are Worried.
You had lost control of yourself.
You are over-thinking.
You have got heartaches.
You hate everyone, even yourself too. Your thoughts are wild.
Your soul is Leaving your body.
You are in constant battle with yourself.
Unfortunately! You cannot escape.
This is what depression did to you. So now, let yourself rest in peace.

Did It ever?

Did it ever happen to you, that you loved, and were loved by someone strongly but in the end, popped up the reasons to be apart?

Fall!

When Dry leaves fall; it reminds me that nothing lasts
forever.
One and all in the sphere, perishes,
Decamp from its Exuberance.

Moon Glows Lonely

Dark is the world, silver is your shine,
Tell me what to hold, as you enshrine?
Silver shade is brightest in the dark night.
Tell me, have you ever seen anything bright?
Not the gold grabs all that does silver shade
All away from grudge and fade,
Dense and refreshing...
On the touch of light, look how it goes,
 Through the whole, like a moon lonely glow.

Save Your Heart, Princess!

They say don't expect, for that hurts.
How to explain that life is also an expectation.
Covert, seems cool in a motivational album.
That a person can survive loneliness,
Only to fill the pot of emptiness.
They say never disclose your life to someone.
How to explain, it seems cool in poetry,
that a heart can carry a sky alone,
This is the greatest truth, supposedly.
They say don't get affected, just go with the flow.
How to explain this, that flow suits the water furious
and slow, for there is certain bliss.
So dear princess, confess, save Your heart Princess
You can never stop expecting, for life is an act
Darling, savour the gifts that you were neglecting.

You are Presence in A Poem!

O! My dearest friend!
I don't understand how to attend.
Such is your presence in a poem short
While you bind a degree of high thought.
Broad mind, winsome look, Beautiful and kind, a chapter of a book, how wondrous you are to me?
And you harmoniously call me ANNI.
Though; you can't be expressed in words
Because you have a place inwards.
Your ways of making me laugh, full in style from the half.
Your presence here is so dear
I know, you like your sleek hair.
You withstand my inner glory.
A flower in this garden of life, accompanying through rife and strife,
To me, a friend loyal, thriving in core, in the great ways of time
I adore the flourishing heart of you.

Bruv!

The one who holds my hand, No matter what I have said,
The one who laughs with me and helps me to find my way,
The one who lives with me, one with whom I play.
The one who listens my stupid talks, without telling me to stop.
The one who always encourages me and sees me on top. The one who is my kind friend & the greatest support.
The one who always wants me to smile and succeed
The one I rely on, when problems stand in my way,
The one whose love always helped me to grow up again' and sway. The one who is happy, faithful and true,
No matter what happens to me I know I have You.

Scarred Soul

Her face was a load of scratches, gapes and cracks along,
Her eyes were smiling sincerely
Like nothing was wrong;
like sundered petals from the rose
Her lips and cheeks were pasty sunken,
The rose had declined, as I went close,
But scent did covertly flow.
She was the kind of girl who searched for love that could never be found,
Those she loved, never put her up...only dropped to unforgiving ground.

The Hearts!

When the Hearts collapse,
There is a thunder and storm
The earth gets lapsed
In one more form.

Now Apart.

How Strange that when we were together, I always
thought that I pay you not much respect and now
apart, I feel like keeping you above everything!
The mere idea of separation turns me blind,
I need something strong to distract my mind.

My Sky Collapsed

And when you're gone and my sky collapsed
 The soul screamed,
The world got lapsed
And our song was redeemed.

Frame of Mind

After Burning all my desires, I Prayed for a little rain. So, Ashes can help me in writing the rhymes of this love again.

I am a woman!

Heaven is beneath my Feet,
I am "Lal" Example of patience,
Habba khatoon, an example of pain.
My father's turban and my mother's proud.
I am a Woman, let me Shout.
I am the mother of Alexander the Great
I give birth to heroes, See My magic
For I have power to change the fate
I can drive everyone crazy with those melodious tunes,
I can Fire up the World While putting Medicine to my Wounds.

Around 3 am

At the time when stars light up my heart, I speak truth
to myself.
3 am thoughts are just pure.
since I start being honest with my Soul.
Am I lonely or loved?
That's the Confusion?
Alas!
I am wasting my life.
Something is haunting me at that sore time. Hopefully
the stars will open a Door for me, and welcome me to
the world of constellations.

Happiest Depressed Soul!

Yeah, I am in a war, war against my own self.
Every dream is a punishment.
Depression is a Murderer; it murders your inner peace.
It's a thief, because it stole my positive thoughts.
It killed the happiest soul I used to be.
It killed the flower that once used to bloom.
It cursed the ocean that was once considered so deep
 It made me dead and I am now a wandering soul.
Crying and Screaming, it killed the Strongest Girl.
I am drowning, not able to find my shore.
I am living in a never-ending pain.
Like a dead body awaiting its coffin
My dreams are lost, my confidence shattered
My body is numb and losing its charm
I tried a lot to win but, not all the battles you fight, you win?

I whole heartedly thank to all the good readers who unfold this last page of book. Thank you for giving your valuable time to the untold musings of my heart.

Flairs and Glairs, a platform by a student for the students. We are esteemed youth struggling to carve out our path for our future and we follow a basic mindset Since everyone is not born with all-round skills. Joining hands with people who are born to execute it with perfection is the best way to evolve. Self-Evolution is the need of the hour but, evolving as a community is what we strive for. The initiative as kickstarted by, Founder- Mr. Shubham Shah with the motive to utilize the skillset and talent of writing has now a team of 10+ people who are actively participating into newer forms of learning and discovering talents among youngsters. We Provide platform and services like Publishing opportunities, Open mics, Workshops, Hands-on training. Operating with Brand Name of Flairs and Glairs (Publication House), we offer the chance of elevating a passionate writer to an esteemed author With Brand name Teekhe Zasbaaat. We bring to you an opportunity to get accustomed with the Public Speaking and Presenting of Thoughts along with regular challenges to brush up your inking spirit. The newest initiative to extend our services we introduced in a new writing Platform- The Glittering Fables and Ink Over Tears.

We Choose to Fly Like A Falcon than to be

a Leg Pulling Crab.

To Know More: Infoline – 7781900870
Mail Us At-
flairsandglairs@gmail.com / info@flairsandglairs.in
Or Visit is at
www.flairsandglairs.com / www.flairsandglairs.in
Social Handles- @flairsandglairs @teekhezasbaaat